"I have read HOLMES & W/
riveted from first page to la
interrelationship of Holmes
than Doyle ever bothered and gives Watson an
absolutely fair shake – and has a mystery, too. Bravo!"

-- Isaac Asimov

"This play has smarts and guts and grins and even a
little blood ... Shackleford's dialogue is clever and
convincing, decorated with smart retorts and sly
innuendo ..."

-- *The Birmingham News*

"Bravo! Fine play!"

-- Jeremy Brett

"The elements of the partnership (not a one-sided
sycophancy) of Holmes and Watson are revealed,
discussed and, to some extent, resolved in this play. It
says many things that Sherlockians have longed to say
and it touches the heart of the relationship between
the Master and his 'Boswell.' The play is well-polished
and its dialog shows the effect of detailed attention.
Arguments on both sides are well-stated, pithy and
thoughtful. The resolutions reached are reasonable
and fitted to the characters. In the hands of a
competent director and talented actors it should be a
real joy to watch and a source of much satisfaction to
Sherlockians."

-- Pastiche expert Philip K. Jones

On the cover: Alan Gardner and Lee Shackleford in the
Library Theatre production. Photo by Elizabeth Adkisson.

HOLMES & WATSON

a play by Lee Shackleford

HOLMES & WATSON was originally presented at the University of Alabama at Birmingham on May 2-6, 1989 as the winner of the Ruby Lloyd Apsey National Play Search. The production was directed by Bob Funk, with scenic design by Melissa Shafer and costume design by Cynthia Turnbull-Langley. The cast was as follows:

SHERLOCK HOLMES   Jack Cannon
JOHN WATSON   Alan Gardner

The off-Broadway production opened at the Theatre at Saint Peter's on January 4, 1990. It was presented by Bernard Block and Associates and was again directed by Bob Funk. Scenic and lighting design was by Kel Laeger, and the cast was as follows:

SHERLOCK HOLMES   Lee Eric Shackleford
JOHN WATSON   Alan Gardner

In the spring of 1891,
the great detective Sherlock Holmes
and his nemesis Professor Moriarty
battled to the death atop the towering peaks
of the Reichenbach Falls in Switzerland.

Each man was intent on
the destruction of the other.

Both were successful.

HOLMES & WATSON

for Bernard

The play takes place in the
sitting room at 221B, Baker Street.

ACT ONE

Scene One
About 7 p.m., April 4th, 1894.

Scene Two
About 11:30 p.m.

ACT TWO

Scene One
An instant later.

Scene Two
About 7 a.m., April 5th, 1894.

ACT ONE

Scene One

The second-story sitting room at #221 Baker Street.

The room is dark but for the large central window, through which the hazy glow of streetlamps filters up from below.

The door to the stairs opens to reveal the handsome, athletic silhouette of WATSON. With the familiar ease of many years' practice, he reaches through the dark and turns the gas-lamps up one by one.

Now the bizarre trappings of this room become visible: a stack of correspondence transfixed to the mantle by a jacknife; an antique Persian slipper out-of-place at the fireplace; the initials "V.R." blasted into the wall with

bullet-holes ... all this and
more, as this Watson has
recorded in his world-famous
writings.

Watson pulls a velvet cord
near the mantle and a bell
sounds, below. Then he
moves to his desk and
removes the cover from a
brand-new Edison cylinder
recorder. He installs a
cylinder and starts the drive
shaft turning.

Then, a sudden thought
interrupts.

                    WATSON
That's very unlike her ...

                    He moves to the door, calls
                    downstairs.

                    WATSON
Mrs. Hudson?

                    No reply.

                    WATSON
Ah. Well, I had hoped for solitude anyway...

                    He returns to the machine,
                    starts it up, and speaks into
                    the recorder.

WATSON

This is John H. Watson. The date is ... April 4th,
1894. This will be, uh ... the first of ...

> He shuts off the machine.
> Watson moves to discard the
> aborted recording, but his
> curiosity wins: he has to
> listen to it first.

WATSON'S VOICE

This is John H. Watson. The date is ... April 4th,
1894. This will be, uh ... the first of ...

WATSON

Good Lord. Surely I don't sound like that.

> He sets this ruined cylinder
> aside and devotes a moment
> to practicing more resonant
> speech. After this "warmup"
> he starts again with a new
> cylinder.

WATSON

This is John Watson. The date is April 4th, 1894. My
great friend and, uh, literary agent, Arthur Conan
Doyle, has been good enough to lend me this device
toward our goal of producing a new book together, a
complete memoir of my life, my experiences, with the
... late Mr. Sherlock Holmes. I have given the world a
record of my friend's struggle against the vast network
of crime in London, a web of evil masterminded by
Professor Moriarty, the "Napoleon of Crime." And
although my public may wish to hear more details
about the final conflict between these two giants, I
must beg them to understand that I have already told
all I know, since I was not an actual witness to the

3

fierce battle between Holmes and Moriarty atop the perilous cliffs at Reichenbach. But it was I alone who found the footprints and other residue which plainly indicated that both Moriarty and Holmes had plunged to their deaths, each succeeding in ... exterminating the other.

> Watson switches the machine off, unable for a moment to go on speaking. He recovers his composure and resumes:

WATSON

So. It is not my intent to elaborate on the death of Mr. Holmes, but rather on his life. I wish to give the world a clearer and more colorful portrait of the best and wisest man I have ever known. It is my hope that this recording device will help me to organize my thoughts, and my first impression is that it seems to be working very well.

> He turns off the machine, and switches to the "listening" mode -- but is interrupted by a sharp sound: the door downstairs opens and closes.

WATSON

Ah, there she is.

> He goes to the door, opens it and calls down the stairs.

WATSON

Mrs. Hudson? I'd very much like to be left undisturbed tonight, so if anyone ...

He stops when he hears a
limping clomp-clomp on the
stairs.

                    WATSON
Who's there?

The clumping stops, then
resumes.

Watson closes the door,
hurries to his desk, and
retrieves his old service
revolver. Gun at the ready,
he returns to the door and
flings it open.

An OLD MAN is revealed.
His back is arched and his
limbs twisted; when he
speaks it is in a strange
croaking voice. His top hat
and coat are dusty and
tattered and his straggly
white beard nearly obscures
his face. He carries a
number of cobwebby books.

                OLD BOOK MAN
You're surprised to see me, sir.

                WATSON
Oh. You're the man I bumped into on the street. I'm
terribly sorry. I'm afraid I was ... not at polite as I
should have --

OLD BOOK MAN

Ah, no, don't fret yourself, sir. It was I who behaved badly, and that's why I've come to call on you. I brought you these as a sort of --

WATSON

No, you make too much of a --

OLD BOOK MAN

You see, I wanted to assure you that if I was a bit gruff earlier there was not any harm meant, and that I am obliged to you for picking up my books.

WATSON

So you followed -- ?

OLD BOOK MAN

No, no, no need for that. No need. I know you, Dr. Watson, everybody knows you. Great friend of that Mr. Sherlock Holmes. He's dead now, you know. But I recalled as how you once lived with him at number two-two-one Baker Street, and considered how you might still drop in on the old place from time to time...

> Suddenly the Old Book Man closes the drapes over the big window.

WATSON

Look here --

OLD BOOK MAN

Well, you don't want those open in the night, do you, sir? I mean, you don't want people looking in, now do you? There are odd people abroad in London, sir -- some of them mad as hatters, sir.

WATSON

That much is clear.

OLD BOOK MAN

Now, I'd rest easier about the earlier unpleasantness if you'd accept these --

WATSON

Oh, I couldn't --

OLD BOOK MAN

-- I insist, sir, I insist. There, there's *British Birds*, and Catullus, and -- what is this? Ah, *The Holy War*. I fancy these three will just fill that gap on the second shelf there. Please take them with my compliments, sir. I shan't leave 'till you've tried them out in that empty space. Hate to see an empty spot on anybody's bookshelf. Like a best friend gone out of their lives.

> Watson takes the books and turns to slip them onto the shelf. As he turns away, the Old Book Man pulls off his whiskers and hat -- and sheds twenty of his sixty years while adding a foot of lean stature to his previous five.
>
> Merriment glistens in the eyes of SHERLOCK HOLMES.

> Watson, meanwhile, is
> dumbfounded to find that
> with only a slight adjustment
> the three books do fit
> perfectly into the space.

WATSON

These volumes do fit precisely! How the devil --

HOLMES

Now, if you already have those, I can return them.

> Watson stares for a moment,
> then sinks in a faint.

HOLMES

Oh dear. And I thought he'd be pleased to see me.

> Holmes leaps for the
> decanter and pours out a
> glass of brandy. He brings it
> back to Watson just as the
> doctor is recovering his
> senses. Watson takes the
> glass and drains its
> contents.

WATSON

That's odd ... I don't recall --

HOLMES

My dear Watson, I owe you a thousand apologies.

> Watson pulls himself back
> up.

WATSON

You ... but ... I ... I ... you ...

HOLMES

Yes. It's good to see that three years have done
nothing to impair your well-known gift of
self-expression.

> Watson walks around
> Holmes, studying him from
> all sides.

WATSON

It is ... really ... you?

HOLMES

Well, who else would it be? I shall tell you all about it
when you stop dancing about me as if I were a
maypole.

> Watson watches as Holmes
> wanders around the
> sitting-room.

HOLMES

The old flat has been well-preserved, I must say. I had
hoped I could return to these rooms and find them
precisely as I left them, and I am not disappointed.
Here and there I see a trace of occasional occupation,
but your visits here seem to have caused no
permanent damage.

> Holmes notices Watson still
> staring at him.

HOLMES

Watson, you look like something dragged in on the
fisherman's net. Speak.

WATSON

Holmes. You are supposed to be dead!

HOLMES

Pardon me if I take exception to that. And as I am
obviously not dead, surely you may now cease to stare
at me as if I were some Dickensian apparition.

WATSON

What I mean to say is ... you told me -- in Switzerland
three years ago -- you planned to sacrifice yourself to
rid the world of Moriarty. That was your plan. A plan
you clearly and obviously carried it out.

HOLMES

That was indeed my plan.

WATSON

Well?

HOLMES

I changed my mind. Ah, now this must be your doing
-- fresh pipe tobacco in the old Persian slipper. Mrs.
Hudson would not be so meticulous as to keep
perishables as part of this ... museum. I surmise --

WATSON

Holmes! I saw your footprints -- and Moriarty's --
leading up to the edge of that terrible precipice --
hundreds of feet to the rocks below!

HOLMES

You did. And the late Professor Moriarty had led a
rather sedentary life, whereas I have studied Japanese
wrestling. I slipped out of his grip and forced him over
the precipice to his death.

WATSON

But you did not fall yourself.

HOLMES

I very nearly did. But I soon made my way back to solid ground -- and into a new world, one in which I was presumed dead. The opportunity of a lifetime, Watson -- the chance to completely re-invent oneself. To go where one likes, do as one pleases, unfettered by one's past.

WATSON

I see. So that ... those are the events as they transpired.

HOLMES

The bare facts. I expect you will clothe them garishly with florid adjectives when you retell my story in your typically melodramatic manner.

WATSON

I am so delighted at finding you to be alive, I cannot complain about your mocking my avocation.

HOLMES

All in the spirit of constructive criticism, old fellow. I've been reading your stories as they've appeared in various periodicals over the last three years. Each more romantic and unscientific than the last. When you relate the account of a mystery we solved together, it is not enough for you to simply state the facts of the case. Your narrative must pause to describe the opalescent glow of the setting sun, dappling the lawn with shimmering purple shadows. Dreadful.

WATSON

Still firm in your rejection of the gentler emotions.

HOLMES

I am fixed; I do not change.

WATSON

So you can honestly say, as you look around these
rooms you and I shared for so many years, amidst all
these relics and mementoes of a hundred thrilling
adventures, for the first time since 1891 -- you feel
nothing.

HOLMES

I would not say that I feel nothing. Let us say that I
feel ... very little.

WATSON

Look. Your old dressing-gown. How many hours have
you spent in this room, wrapped in this beloved
garment while puzzling over the solution to a mystery
where the lives of countless people hang in the
balance? Don't you feel a sort of electric sensation
rushing through your body when you see this again
after three years ... smell it, touch its familiar,
comfortable fabric?

HOLMES

I do feel something. I feel I should put this on as there
is a definite draft in this room.

WATSON

Well. I still thank the Lord you are alive.

HOLMES

Do you? Even if my return has placed you in danger?

WATSON

Danger?

HOLMES

Yes, does that frighten you?

WATSON

Certainly not. But danger from whom? Moriarty is
dead.

HOLMES

Yes. But the "first lieutenant" of his criminal army is
not. He alone witnessed the entire struggle at
Reichenbach. He alone has shared the secret that
Moriarty did not drag me down into the abyss when he
fell.

WATSON

Good Lord.

HOLMES

This man has dogged my tracks for three years -- and
yes, I am sure he has followed me here. He will shoot
me at the next clear opportunity, and Colonel
Sebastian Moran ... never misses.

WATSON

Has he never tried to avenge himself on you before?

HOLMES

Frequently, at first. But as the years went by I became
more adept at acquiring new names and new
occupations. I believe that sometime last year he had
given up on me entirely. But meanwhile his agents
have been watching these rooms, night after night for
months. They had often observed lights and shadows
from within. Moran surmised that this nocturnal
visitor must be his old nemesis, the fugitive consulting
detective -- when all the while it was merely a
physician filling his idle hours by writing
sensationalist prose.

WATSON

But if there is some danger that Colonel Moran is laying a trap for you, why in the world did you come here?

HOLMES

To lay a trap for him. That will require us both to remain here until morning, I'm afraid, but --

WATSON

We -- WE will capture Colonel Moran? Tonight? Holmes, this is -- this is like a dream given shape. I -- I stand ready to help you any way I can! You have only to instruct me.

HOLMES

Then here are my instructions. Stay out of my way.

WATSON

Holmes ...

HOLMES

My dear Watson. You do not understand how dangerous a man is this assassin, this Colonel Sebastian Moran. He is one of the most famous big-game hunters in Europe. An authority on stalking elusive prey. I know that he will establish himself somewhere that allows a clear view of this building -- and the instant he is convinced I am in his sights he will shoot with his world-renowned accuracy. Now, when he makes that attempt, our friends from the regular police will close in and clap him in irons once and for all. Until then --

WATSON

There are policemen watching this street?

HOLMES

Get away from that window! For God's sake, Watson,
try to muster some glimmer of common sense.

WATSON

Holmes. I can't begin to tell you how delighted I am to
find that you are alive and well after all this time. And
in this current crisis I am as eager as ever to stand by
your side. But I see no reason for you to--

HOLMES

Oh, come now, old fellow -- you know I never mean
anything I say. Now tell me about your life of the last
three years. Apart from what I have deduced logically,
which is that you have been visiting Baker Street
several times a week, and on each occasion for several
hours.

WATSON

That's not deduction, Holmes. Those spies of Colonel
Moran's reported they saw lights and shadows. Not
exactly proof that it was I who was here.

HOLMES

I speak of the fresh pipe tobacco and the half-dozen
other clues which should be readily apparent to
anyone. You've been here and you've been writing.
The evidence is all around us.

WATSON

All around us.

HOLMES

Certainly. You have brought in one of the new
cylinder-recorders, which you have no doubt been
using for dictation. And your blotter bears a distinct
impression from the recent use of a sharpened
pen-point.

WATSON

Fair enough.

HOLMES

And look at our bedraggled old floor-rug. It has been beaten out recently -- by Mrs. Hudson, I expect -- but there are impressions of a man's boot here -- and here -- the same footprint but at different depths and angles, and in fact slightly overlapping. And over here on the bare floor is the faintest trace of the same footprint, made after it had trodden in rainwater -- which it could not have done today -- while over here by the door, the same footprint is etched in extremely dry and powdery dust. All of these prints match the boots you are wearing at this very moment. Ergo, you have been here more than once in recent days.

WATSON

Well. If you are quite finished with your deductions --

HOLMES

Finished? Wouldn't you like to know why I believe your medical practice has been doing well, in fact perhaps too well -- that some time ago you began allowing your wife to determine your grooming habits -- and that since I last saw you, there has been an increase in your daily intake of tea, and that you have become substantially more sentimental?

WATSON

Holmes --

HOLMES

And finally, that we shall have rain tomorrow?

WATSON

I had almost forgotten how your gifts of observation
and deduction could be at once fascinating and
infuriating. You have not been here ten minutes and
already ...

HOLMES

Then you admit you are at a loss?

WATSON

I confess I am out of practice. Fire when ready.

HOLMES

Very well. Your recent success I can plainly see from
your hat-band, which is almost worn through from the
frequent removal and replacement of the stethoscope
tube you carry there. The hat is quite new and
therefore should not bear so deep an impression as
this unless the stethoscope had been in constant use.
I said your business has perhaps been "too good"
because the pigmentation of your eyes and
surrounding tissues betrays a paucity of sleep but
abundance of worry.

WATSON

I have a young patient with the scarlet fever. Her
family is having a rather bad time of it.

HOLMES

You see? I know my Watson -- always his neighbor
before himself. And I know your wife was dictating
your grooming habits because I have, after all, spent a
certain portion of my life looking at your moustache
day in and day out without complaint, but your good
lady wife has succumbed to that female obsession with
men's dining habits, and has begged you to trim your
moustache away from your mouth so it does not act as
a sort of sieve when you are eating your soup.

WATSON

You said I had been drinking more tea than before ... ?

HOLMES

The color of your teeth has turned slightly in three
years. I would attribute that to tea or coffee, but I
happen to know your preference for tea.

WATSON

Well.

HOLMES

As to the new sentimentality, I deduce that from the
four trinkets you have attached to your watch-chain ...
it is not a fancy you had affected before -- I see that
you now feel a need to be surrounded by mementoes.

WATSON

A weakness we both share, I may say.

HOLMES

Irrelevant, but yes, you may say it.

WATSON

This method of deduction of yours is as fascinating to
observe as it ever was, I must admit.

HOLMES

I thank you. But aren't you going to ask me --

WATSON

Yes, very well, Holmes, how the devil do you know
from observing me that it will rain tomorrow?

HOLMES

Ah! You see, you have become so accustomed to your
old war injury ...

WATSON

Ah --

HOLMES

I perceive that you are limping tonight, albeit slightly.
And the wound always hurt you --

HOLMES and WATSON

-- when the weather is about to change.

HOLMES

It was bright and sunny today, therefore, it will rain
tomorrow. Where is the mystery in all this?

> He throws himself into a
> chair and lights the pipe.

HOLMES

By the by, since we were speaking of your wife, won't
she be concerned when you don't come home tonight?

> Watson turns away from
> Holmes, deliberately hiding
> his face.

HOLMES

Oh dear.

WATSON

Mary died ... rather suddenly. We never even really
knew what ... what was ...

HOLMES

I cannot tell you how sorry I am. And I never knew her
well.

WATSON

No ... you never took the time.

HOLMES

No.

WATSON

Do you see that I had lost the two most ... the two
people who --

HOLMES

Yes, I do see what you mean, but then was then and
now is now and we are both here, are we not? With a
million new problems to divert us and to challenge us
... whatever has gone before, tonight we are where you
and I belong, in danger for our lives as always!

Watson stares at him.

WATSON

Holmes, where in hell have you been for the last three
years?

HOLMES

It really is remarkable, the work Mrs. Hudson has
done in preserving and maintaining --

WATSON

I see no reason to avoid my question.

HOLMES

My dear fellow, I have no desire to be brusque, but you
know my opinion of your written accounts of our
adventures together. I have no intention of my years
alone becoming the source of a ... penny-dreadful.

WATSON

Penny-dreadful! Really, Holmes, I --

HOLMES

I admit the term was poorly-chosen. Listen. Perhaps you've heard or read of the adventures of a Norwegian explorer named Sigerson?

WATSON

Well, as a matter of fact --

HOLMES

He was none other than my humble self. Let your imagination work with that. By all means, give him some adventures in the Far East.

WATSON

You were in the Far East!

HOLMES

I did not say that. I proposed the Far East as a romantic setting for one of your stories.

WATSON

Holmes. If you will not tell me where you have been, at least tell me why you did not notify me as soon as possible that you were alive?

HOLMES

It has only now become possible. I have had no contact as myself with anyone except my brother Mycroft since 1891.

WATSON

Mycroft knew. All along.

HOLMES

Yes, and this morning I had the amusement of alarming our good Mrs. Hudson, and of warning her to stay away from these premises for at least a day. You should have seen her face --

He finally sees the look
Watson has been giving him.

HOLMES
I acted in the best interest of all parties concerned.
You may believe me or not, as you choose.

Silence.

WATSON
Do you remember when you pretended to have a fatal
illness, for the sake of luring your would-be murderer
into these rooms?

HOLMES
Ah, yes. That was a rather clever ruse, though I say it
who shouldn't.

WATSON
Yes. You thoroughly convinced everyone that you had
only hours to live. And you refused to let me, as a
physician, to treat you. You said I hadn't the skill.

HOLMES
And later I explained that this was all part of the
deception. If you had examined me, you would have
seen that I was not a dying man at all!

WATSON
Nonetheless, you lied to me -- and insulted me as well!
If you had been any other man in the world, I might
very well have given you a pounding you would not
soon forget.

HOLMES
It was part of the trap, Watson. I knew that an honest
man such as yourself could not deceive our prey ...
now, I, on the other hand ...

WATSON

So now you've done it again ... this time causing me to grieve for three years to serve your purposes.

HOLMES

And see how successfully it worked! Everyone in the world has believed me dead -- because you believed it.

WATSON

Yes, for the love of God, Holmes, think of them! Look at these letters -- they all arrived here for you in the first year after your "death." I'm sure a large part of it is entreaties for help from people who had not yet read of your demise -- people who needed you, Holmes! And you turned your back on them --

HOLMES

May I remind you that it was on their behalf that I risked my life to destroy Professor Moriarty? I assure you that because I personally rid this nation of a criminal mastermind, every one of those poor souls sleeps more soundly tonight.

WATSON

Unless, of course, they have since died.

HOLMES

In which case they sleep even more soundly than the rest. Hm! Here is an interesting specimen, however -- from the King of Bohemia. Letter of condolence to you, I expect. Do you remember the little problem in which we were able to give him some assistance? That was a fine case.

WATSON

If I remember correctly, we were of very little use to the King of Bohemia. That was a case you lost.

HOLMES

Well, yes.

WATSON

To a woman.

HOLMES

Not at all, my good fellow ... to *the* woman. You know better than that. Clever, brave, brilliant Irene Adler.

WATSON

Encouraging to see that you've not forgotten her at least. Do you still have the sovereign she gave you?

> Holmes shows it; it is
> attached to his watch-chain.

WATSON

And you scoffed at my trinkets before.

HOLMES

Not at all.

WATSON

At any rate, that was as close as the world ever came to seeing the aloof, dispassionate Sherlock Holmes in love.

HOLMES

No, the so-called fair sex has always been your department -- to the extent that you completely misunderstand my admiration for Irene Adler's intelligence and audacity. Well, it will be interesting to sort through all of this. Like archaeology, eh? Dig down through the layers of time. Hm ... Here's a package from my friend Benjamin Alexander.

WATSON

Benjamin Alexander? The shipping magnate?

HOLMES

Why, yes ... how do you know him?

As an answer Watson finds a
copy of the *Times*. He hands
the paper to Holmes, who
reads the headline with
delight.

HOLMES

Murdered! This is ... yesterday's paper. So this
happened the day before! Incredible. We met several
years ago when I was of some small service to him.
"Benjamin Alexander, president of the Alexander
Imports empire, is dead at the age of fifty-nine. The
circumstances seem to indicate foul play." Oh, this is
excellent, Watson!

WATSON

"Excellent"?

HOLMES

Of course! Just what you and I need to while away our
evening of captivity!

WATSON

Holmes, the man has died. A friend of yours, you said.

HOLMES

I grieve for him in my own way, Watson. Perhaps we
may be able to aid in finding his murderer, hm? This
says he was discovered "by his son, James Alexander,
at half past eight last night. Young Alexander said he
ran to his father's study after hearing cries for help in
his father's voice. When he reached the room his

father lay dead on the floor, a hundred-pound note near his left hand." Hmm! "The dead man's throat was mottled with reddish marks as if great pressure had been applied upon it. The butler, Samson Menninger, was also in the room when young Alexander arrived. Menninger was in a nearly hysterical state and proclaimed his innocence loudly." Well, I should think so. "Alexander stated that his father's cries seemed to him to be pleas against an attack of some kind, and had about them a distinct strangling sound. Even at that, the cries were loud enough to be heard over the "1812 Overture", a recording of which Alexander, Senior, was playing at the time on one of the new gramophone machines." What a ghastly sound that must have been! "The case is being investigated by Scotland Yard's Inspector Lestrade -- " Oh dear! " -- the famous criminologist!" Ha! -- who at once arrested Menninger on the charge of willful murder. It does seem to stand against Menninger that Benjamin Alexander had recently reduced the salaries of his entire household staff." Well. Knowing Lestrade, I don't doubt he barged in, heard the one account and none other, then threw this butler into prison, priding himself on a job well done. On the other hand, of course --

                           WATSON
Holmes.

                           HOLMES
Yes?

                           WATSON
Surely it would be helpful to, eh ... open the package.

                           HOLMES
Aha! A most excellent suggestion.

WATSON

It arrived not long after I returned from Switzerland ...
and in all the confusion of those days ... wait, there is
an envelope that was tied to the package ... ah, here.

HOLMES

This wrapping paper is milled bamboo. Obviously from
Venezuela.

WATSON

Such paper could be made any number of places.

HOLMES

I happen to know this type of paper comes from
Venezuela, so I'll wager the package does as well. And
it was brought through the rain, for at least part of its
journey. It has been the source of amusement of a
good many people who have handled it ... see the
variety of finger-smudges here? While on its journey it
must have been examined by anyone who came within
a yard of it. It was addressed by Alexander himself,
and not a secretary, indicating highly personal
contents.

WATSON

And how do you know that?

HOLMES

I recall that he was left-handed as this handwriting
obviously is.

WATSON

Couldn't a secretary just as easily be left-handed?

HOLMES

And scribble his employer's name in this way? No,
ruining one's own name in print is a very personal
privilege. Well ... let's open it and see what my late
friend had sent me.

They open it, peer inside.

HOLMES

Good God.

He pulls out a small glass
bottle packed with white
powder.

WATSON

At least a hundred of them.

Holmes taps a bit onto his
finger, tastes it.

WATSON

Cocaine.

HOLMES

Enough to supply a casual user for years. Even a
serious addict for many months.

He reads a note from the
envelope.

HOLMES

"My dear Holmes -- I told you I would find a way to
repay you for the help you gave in proving my wife's
innocence in that little matter -- "

WATSON

What "little matter"? You never --

He takes the letter, reads
aloud.

WATSON
" -- in that little matter, and after reading the story
your biographer Dr. Watson called *The Sign of the Four*
I knew this would be the perfect gift. This is a share of
a gift from Mr. Jacob Freeman, my manager of imports
in ..."

HOLMES
Go on.

WATSON
"... in Venezuela. He has sent me a supply that should
last many years to come. I thought it only fair to share
with you." Good Heavens. "Please never divulge
Freeman as the source except to order more of the
same. Gratefully, Benjamin Alexander."

HOLMES
A pretty little prize.

WATSON
So Alexander used cocaine. And sent dangerous drugs
through the post, where it might easily have fallen into
the hands of innocent persons.

HOLMES
You speak as if the sale of cocaine should be
prohibited.

WATSON
It should!

HOLMES
I would have thought that your old stand on that issue
would have changed by now.

WATSON

As a medical professional, I am more firmly opposed to it than ever. Like most addictive drugs, it is extremely unpredictable. I am confident that the majority will soon agree. The benefits do not outweigh its --

HOLMES

Yes, yes -- thank you -- but for the time being, fortunately, it is widely available for all to do with as they please.

WATSON

Well, that will change one day soon.

HOLMES

Possibly, but even before that I should not be surprised if its use becomes even more commonplace. It might appear, say, in various foods -- or as a cold beverage of some sort. Wouldn't that be marvelous? Well, I assure you it would be very popular. In any event, I shall treat the late Mr. Alexander's gift with the respect it deserves ... moreso, for his untimely demise. Which, by the way, troubles me greatly.

WATSON

Holmes ... you don't still indulge ... do you?
                    (receiving no answer)
Holmes.

HOLMES

Very infrequently.

WATSON

I should hope not at all! God only knows what ill effects --

HOLMES

You have already favored me with your views on the
subject. But can you honestly say that I appear any
the worse for my habits?

WATSON

I would say you are not the same man I knew three
years ago.

HOLMES

This is the result of your shabby powers of
observation. I retain one hundred per-cent of my
accustomed stamina. I daresay few men of our age
can truly say that.

WATSON

There's my point, Holmes. Since I saw you last, we
have both celebrated our fortieth birthdays --

HOLMES

If "celebrated" is the proper word.

WATSON

-- when the body begins to slow, we become less
durable, less resistant to illnesses ...

HOLMES

You speak of typical men. Ordinary men.

WATSON

If you don't believe me when I say you are carelessly
tampering with your own body, at least have some pity
on me. I have lived with the picture in my mind of
your ... corpse. I can see it all too clearly now, at the
bottom of that waterfall, or here, dead from this
horrible drug.

HOLMES

My corpse? Old fellow, I --

WATSON

I cannot erase from my mind the image of your body,
lying on the rocks hundreds of feet below me. Of
course I never saw any such thing ... but my
imagination served to curse me with the picture.

HOLMES

Hazard of being a highly imaginative writer.

WATSON

I suppose so. But it took little imagination to think of
you as I last saw you ... in your deerstalker cap and
Inverness cloak ... as most who knew you seem to
remember you.

HOLMES

Oh! That reminds me! There should be a package
here only a few days old, with no return address.

WATSON

Oh, yes ... I had wondered about that!

> Holmes opens it hastily,
> takes out the deerstalker cap
> and Inverness cloak they
> were just discussing.

WATSON

Of course. Now you are complete, I suppose. I must
confess curiosity almost got the better of me with this
package as well.

> Watson searches the inside
> of the box for any further
> treasures.

HOLMES

I had Mycroft keep these, all this while ... a few days
ago I asked him to send them here to await my arrival.
I had decided I should need them again.

> He shoulders into the cape
> and drops the cap onto his
> head -- then sprawls on the
> floor as if he had fallen there
> from a great height.

HOLMES

So you were envisioning something like this?

> Watson looks up from the
> box to see the very image of
> his nightmares.

WATSON

Holmes, for God's sake!

HOLMES

Oh. My apologies, old man. I forget your fragile and
sensitive nature.

WATSON

You really are ... utterly devoid of human emotion.

HOLMES

Well, I do try. But we are ignoring the problem at
hand.

WATSON

Colonel Moran?

HOLMES

Heavens, no. We shall hear from the Yard tomorrow
that he has been captured, I am sure. No, I refer to
the Alexander murder.

WATSON

I confess I am interested as well ... but what can we
do? We cannot visit the scene. Even if we could, any
clues would be two days old.

HOLMES

I think this extraordinary twist of Fate may have
placed a good many of the clues in our hands here.
Besides, what else have we to do? We must keep a
vigil here ... we may as well make some productive use
of the time.

WATSON

Well. It won't be the first time we worked throughout
the night on such a problem.

HOLMES

By no means.

WATSON

I recall vividly how you often brooded over a problem
for days on end, refusing to sleep or eat ... I never
could understand how you did it.

HOLMES

My constitution has always been a hardy one.

WATSON

I should say so; to look at you one would probably not
guess you bend iron bars with your bare hands.

HOLMES

I never did that.

WATSON

You did.

HOLMES

I have no recollection of it.

WATSON

You did it.

HOLMES

When?

WATSON

Dr. Grimesby Roylott? I called it "The Adventure of the Speckled Band."

HOLMES

I recall the "speckled band." And Roylott.

WATSON

He demonstrated his superior strength by bending our fireplace poker ... and you ... bent it back again.

HOLMES

Nothing to it. Anyone could have done it.

WATSON

Nonsense.

HOLMES

Anyone at all. I have a little theory about the colossal power of the human body when under various kinds of stress, particularly emotional stress.

WATSON

I find that difficult to believe.

HOLMES

Shall I show you how it works? It's really quite
interesting.

WATSON

If you don't mind my asking, Holmes, what could you
possibly know about emotional stress? I have never
observed you responding to any event with any feelings
other than ... self-congratulation.

HOLMES

You exaggerate. But I do pride myself on my control of
my emotions.

WATSON

So I have observed. So I find it difficult to believe that
you can develop a revolutionary theory about their
power.

> Holmes crosses to the
> fireplace and picks up the
> poker.

HOLMES

Here -- bend this.

WATSON

Surely you jest.

HOLMES

At least give it a try, man.

WATSON

... another trick of yours, make me look ridiculous ...

> Watson sets his grip,
> assaults the bar with
> moderate force. Nothing.

36

He tries harder. Still
nothing. He sighs, hands it
to Holmes.

WATSON

Now you do it.

HOLMES

I'm sure I couldn't. This is my point, you see; I'm not
under emotional stress.

WATSON

"At least give it a try, man."

Holmes takes the poker, sets
his grip as Watson did. He is
successful in putting a slight
curve in the bar.

HOLMES

My. Well, I have put a bend in it. Try again -- it should
be easier now that I've started it for you.

Watson tries again. Nothing.

HOLMES

Oh, come now, did they teach you to quit this easily in
the service? Where's that old Army spirit?

Watson tries yet again.

HOLMES

You have gotten out of shape, sitting around here and
at your little office, writing stories about other people's
adventures. But that's just like during the war, isn't
it? One bullet and it's back home for old Watson,
limping around at every change in the weather, looking
for sympathy --

WATSON

Holmes ...

HOLMES

Keep trying! That was your whole problem, man, I'd give you a simple little problem to solve and you'd say, "It cannot be done" or "The solution is hidden to me" -- because you **see** but you do not **observe!** Always rather more on the lookout for the ladies than for the criminals on our little outings.

WATSON
(red-faced from the strain)

If you think --

HOLMES

Then you write your ridiculous music-hall accounts of my cases and cloud the issues with romantic nonsense. It's no wonder you've never made your mark in the world, and that you'll die a penniless anonymous figure, just like your **worthless alcoholic brother!**

This is too much -- Watson roars at Holmes --

WATSON

HOLMES!

HOLMES

Yes?

WATSON

That is enough! I am through with your abuse, your -- your --

>   Watson finally sees that he
>   has bent the poker entirely
>   double.

WATSON
Good Lord in Heaven!

HOLMES
Emotional duress. Quite remarkable, really.

>   Holmes placidly relights his
>   pipe.

WATSON
You said those things ... so I would ...

HOLMES
A very effective demonstration, wouldn't you say?

WATSON
Holmes ... you said some very unkind things.

HOLMES
Oh, surely you don't think I meant any of them? It
was an experiment, a scientific proof to a theory -- I
thought you'd find it diverting.

WATSON
I don't wish to sound over-sensitive, Holmes, but I
think you often blind yourself to other people's
feelings. I can't see that bringing ... my brother's ...
problem into it was at all necessary.

HOLMES
It was crucial! I knew that would be the trigger that
would release your hidden strength! It was the whole
point of the demonstration, arrived at scientifically and
acted on logically.

                    WATSON
Holmes!

                              He hurls the poker away --

                    WATSON
Go to the devil!

                              He marches to the coat-rack
                              and gathers his things --

                    HOLMES
Don't go outside.

                    WATSON
I shall go where I damn well please.

                    HOLMES
Watson, I assure you -- Colonel Moran has wasted no
time finding a position from which to observe this
house and to place our front door in his gun-sights.
Please do not oblige him by going outside.

                              Watson stares at Holmes.
                              Finally:

                    WATSON
If I did not know better, I would say that remark was
the result of a genuine regard that one friend had for
another ... but not from Mr. Sherlock Holmes, the
logical thinking machine! I know that could not be
true. So why don't you want me to go out there?
Would it be somehow inconvenient to you, having my
death on your conscience?

                    HOLMES
Really, Watson. How can you ask such a question?

WATSON

How? Because I have had three years to consider what
my life here with you was like! And despite my deep
respect and admiration for you, I have also realized
that you frequently manipulated me, you insulted me,
you always treated me as an inferior. I have been glad
to show more respect for your abilities than anybody,
but I tell you that I am not your inferior, nor is any
man. I've served the Crown in battle, and now I serve
her Majesty's subjects as doctor. But I am not your
servant.

> He crosses to the twisted
> poker, picks it up.

WATSON

And if you believe I enjoy being a subject of one of your
experiments, you are sadly mistaken!

> A sudden epiphany:

WATSON

Just a moment. Just a moment! When you bent the
other poker, the night Dr. Roylott threatened you, you
must have been under "emotional stress"! You were
actually angry -- or frightened! It's beyond belief.
Sherlock Holmes in a brilliant display of emotional
weakness. A pity no one but I was here to witness it.

> He pauses at his bedroom
> door.

WATSON

There is one thing I would like to know. If you have
never particularly needed my assistance, why in God's
name did you drag me along behind you for a decade
while you made a name for yourself? Or, may I say,
while I made a name for you? Did you simply require
a dim-witted but faithful someone to make you seem
clever by comparison?

> Receiving no answer, Watson
> goes into his room and closes
> the door.
>
> Holmes remains motionless,
> like a statue of himself.
> Suddenly he snatches up the
> fireplace poker, and
> wrenches it back into a
> straight rod.
>
> He hurls the poker across
> the room, throws himself
> into his chair, and stares
> into space.

Scene Two

A few minutes before
midnight. Holmes has
turned most of the gas-lamps
down.

He sits at Watson's desk
now, conducting a minute
examination of the
cylinder-recorder. He pauses
to drink from a
brandy-snifter, then returns
to his study.

He switches the mechanism
on and:

WATSON'S VOICE
This is John H. Watson. The date is ... April 4th,
1894. This will be, uh ... the first of ...

Watson enters from his
room, glowering.

HOLMES
Ah! Watson. I am sorry if I disturbed your rest. I had
no idea the recording would be so amplified.

> Watson apparently ignores
> this. He goes to the brandy
> decanter and pours himself a
> drink.

HOLMES

Yes, by all means, a glass or two of the brandy -- just
what's called for, I find. I was wondering if it was you
or Mrs. Hudson who has filled the old decanter,
because I don't recall our ever having anything quite
so fine as this on hand in the old days.

> Silence from Watson.
> Finally:

WATSON

Any sign of Colonel Moran?

HOLMES

No, there have been no attempts on my life in the last
four hours. And though I recall you are notoriously
difficult to rouse when asleep, I do believe the sound of
a rifled bullet smashing through our window and
striking me down would have stirred even you from
your slumber.

WATSON

I have not slept. I have been sitting in my room
pondering all that has happened tonight, and I have
decided --

HOLMES

My dear Watson -- it has been an extraordinary
evening, one which would strain the nerves of a
Tibetan mystic. If we have exchanged cross words,
you must cast them from you mind and put it all down
to the eccentricities of your old friend. Now come and
tell me about this machine you've acquired.

WATSON

It isn't as simple as that.

HOLMES

I don't know much about it, except that it was
invented by the American, Thomas Alva Edison, in
1877 and utilizes a wax cylinder to record the vibration
pattern produced by the human voice. Can you
enlighten me as to any other facts?

WATSON

Holmes, please ...

HOLMES

I'm asking a very simple question, Watson; you could
answer it. If this device will record and repeat any
voice, any sound ... think what a tool it could be for
us! Much can be learned from a person's voice, word
choices, their vocal mannerisms. This man Edison is
truly a genius. I recall that when we heard of the
invention of the electric lamp I was amazed that an
American had possessed the patience and
determination to do such a marvelous thing -- but
then I realized he must have known it would make him
very wealthy and then I understood. You see, Watson,
in the future, we'll have all of our clients dictate their
little problems into this machine! And we shall
photograph the subjects as well. If we had a camera --

WATSON

That is what I wish to speak to you about.

HOLMES

Photography? Or the recordings?

WATSON

The clients. .

HOLMES

Yes. With the recorder and a camera, we could even
receive cases in absentia, as it were. While we were
out conducting an investigation, a client could tell his
or her problem to our machines, and that much more
work could be done. Wouldn't that be marvelous?

WATSON

Marvelous? You would have some poor soul come to
you, seeking help, and instead find himself speaking to
a -- a mechanical contrivance?

HOLMES

Certainly.

WATSON

I find the very idea nauseating.

HOLMES

You are clouding the fact-gathering process with
emotions, old fellow. We are back to our old
accustomed roles: I the brain and you the heart.

WATSON

There you have described it perfectly.

HOLMES

I thank you.

WATSON

I am not sure I intended that as a compliment.

HOLMES

Ah, a touch, a distinct touch. Well, we need not
"improve" our methods just yet, in any event. We will
have our hands quite full with bringing our old trade
back to its accustomed level of activity.

WATSON

You honestly believe that you and I shall simply
recommence our old partnership, as if these three
years of deception had never occurred?

HOLMES

Old fellow, look around you. We are already at work
on a case, precisely as we were three years ago. Ah!
You've finished your drink -- let me pour you another.

WATSON

I thought we needed to remain alert.

HOLMES

I doubt either of us will overindulge. And we are
reasonably safe as long as we remain here until
morning. So, we make the best of things.

> He hands Watson a drink
> and begins pacing the room
> with the air of a university
> lecturer.

HOLMES

Now the facts are these: Alexander was in his study.
"1812 Overture" on the gramophone. A cry was heard
-- his son rushes in. The son sees the butler, the
gramophone ... most importantly, sees his father, dead
on the floor, with marks on his neck and a
one-hundred-pound note near his left hand.

WATSON

I see it now. You insist on continuing this hopeless
investigation simply to avoid telling me where you have
been and why you came back!

HOLMES

Watson, if this butler Menninger did not kill his
master, then an innocent man has been accused.
Surely it is our duty to come to his aid.

WATSON

Very well, I will make my argument, then withdraw.
Look: what can possibly be amiss in this? You read
that the butler's salary had been reduced. He
obviously went up to his employer's rooms, put on the
loud music to conceal the sounds he knew would
follow ... Alexander attempted to bribe the butler into
peace, and the butler, offended by this insult, leapt for
Alexander and strangled him. Now, the matter is
simplicity itself, as you're so fond of saying.

HOLMES

Are you quite finished?

WATSON

Yes.

HOLMES

Very well. My objections are these. I cannot imagine
a man committing such a murder over such a petty
problem unless he is naturally a violent and impulsive
person ... and I certainly cannot imagine the jovial Mr.
Alexander having ever hired an ill-tempered man as
his personal butler. Further, even an impulsive and
quick-tempered man would not strangle a man with
his bare hands with a house full of people -- potential
witnesses! Not at half past eight in the evening when
they were all probably awake but about some quiet
diversion. Surely he would at least find a quicker,
quieter means.

WATSON

But you are assuming that this was planned.

HOLMES

I do not assume anything. It is a shocking habit to make guesses -- destructive to the logical faculties.

WATSON

Nonsense. Your examination of the problem is rife with assumptions. The murderer may have been an imbecile, or insane, for all we know. Come to that, we assume there was a murder in the first place. This could be a bizarre suicide, for all we know.

HOLMES

Are you suggesting Alexander strangled himself? Watson!

WATSON

Do you see? You asked for my opinion and I was glad to offer it, and now you mock me for it! You have always done this --

HOLMES

Yes, it is a little game I play -- you should know it by now. I am sorry if it has caused you offense.

WATSON

Why is it so hard to believe you?

HOLMES

I'm sure I don't know. But, to be fair, we could put your theory to a sort of test.

WATSON

How?

HOLMES

We shall re-enact the crime. I shall play the role of poor Alexander; you can be your excitable butler.

                    WATSON
I don't think -- -

                    HOLMES
I shall be reading in my study. You enter and surprise
me as per your theory. Oh, come now, don't be shy.

                    WATSON
You mean, we'll say what they might have said, and so
on?

                    HOLMES
Certainly. Let's try it.

                    WATSON
Well ...

                              He goes across the room,
                              then returns, with the
                              demeanor of an angry man
                              with a mission.

                    HOLMES
"What are you doing in here?"

                    WATSON
"I want to talk with you!" I turn on the gramophone ...

                    Watson mimes this.

                    HOLMES
It is loud; they must speak loudly to be heard.
                    (He hums "1812" loudly,
                    in between his spoken lines)
"Turn that off at once!"

WATSON

"Why have you cut my money? I can barely support
myself as it is!"

HOLMES

"It is still more than you deserve, you loafer!"

WATSON

"`Loafer'? I'll kill you for that!"

HOLMES

Come, come, Watson, I don't think he would,
somehow. "Loafer" is not the sort of word that incites
felonies.

WATSON

It was your choice. Let us assume something
sufficiently provoking was said.

HOLMES

Very well. This is your story, after all.

He sings loudly again --

WATSON

Yes. Um ... "How dare you! I'll kill you for that!"

HOLMES

"Now, don't do anything rash, Menninger ... here, if it's
money you want ... how would a hundred be, eh?" I
don't have a note to use for the hundred, do you?

WATSON

Well, I certainly don't have a hundred. Would a fiver
do?

Watson fishes a five-pound
note from his pocket.

51

HOLMES

The five-pound note has slightly different dimensions
than the hundred, of course, which may be significant.
We shall remember it, in any event.

He takes it, holds it flat so
most of it is visible.

HOLMES

"So it's money you want, is it? What about this for a
start?'

WATSON

"You can't buy me like a ... piece of coal, you jackal!"

Watson grabs Holmes by the
throat.

HOLMES

"Help! You're choking me!" You ... ah ... Wat ... really
chok --

WATSON

Oh, Good Lord, I'm sorry. Are you all right?

Pause as Holmes recovers.

HOLMES

Well. Your theory may be right after all. It does seem
to cover all the facts.
(a beat, then)
I doubt seriously, however, that Menninger would have
said, "You can't buy me like a piece of coal, you
jackal."

WATSON

Creative license.

HOLMES

Fair enough. I believe I will have another brandy.

WATSON

At the rate we're drinking, Colonel Moran has only to wait until we collapse, then walk in the front door and put bullets in both our heads.

HOLMES

Should we stop, then?

WATSON

Oh, by no means.

HOLMES

I am glad to hear it. How are you feeling? Are you still angry with me?

WATSON

Yes, but somehow the exact reason is becoming foggy. Strange how charitable one becomes with enough brandy inside.

HOLMES

Absolutely. I believe that moderation should be observed in all things ... including moderation. Let us continue to be immoderate, and before the sun rises we shall be extremely charitable.

WATSON

I didn't say it was making me amnesiac. Don't think I've forgotten the fact that you still refuse to tell me where you've been, or why you didn't let me know you were alive. I haven't forgotten.

HOLMES

Will you trust me when I say that I did what I thought was best?

Pause.

WATSON
Do you know, your abilities as an actor are a liability at times like these. I have no clue as to whether I should believe you or not.

HOLMES
Oh, you flatter me.

WATSON
That was not intended to be complimentary.

HOLMES
Either way, it serves to remind me that I never ascended to any prominence at all as an actor. Perhaps I turned to criminal detection just in time to prevent a calamitous career.

WATSON
I thought you had performed Shakespeare.

HOLMES
Certainly, but there are a great many roles in the plays of the Bard that require absolutely no ability. I was cast in several of those.

WATSON
You played Malvolio.

HOLMES
Ah, yes! The culmination of a boyhood dream, playing in *Twelfth Night.*

WATSON
And surely at some time you played Hamlet.

HOLMES

Alas, no, as much as I longed for it. He is the greatest character in English literature.

WATSON

Nonsense. What about King Arthur?

HOLMES

My dear fellow, I was speaking exclusively of fiction.

WATSON

Hear, hear.

HOLMES

I imagine I am always the actor at heart. Perhaps that's why I felt I had to make my return known to you in such a way that ...

WATSON

That frightened me out of my wits?

HOLMES

Well, yes.

WATSON

It was very effective.

HOLMES

Though not, actually, one of my best disguises. You've never seen me as an old woman -- I'm quite convincing.

WATSON

I'm sure you are. You are quite expert at concealing your identity. So much so that one might live under the same roof with you for years and never know who you are.

HOLMES

Precisely.

WATSON

Do you know any of *Hamlet*?

HOLMES

Quite a bit, why?

WATSON

I think I should like to see you in that role.

HOLMES

Perhaps someday.

WATSON

I meant tonight.

HOLMES

Now? Here?

WATSON

You have a pressing engagement elsewhere?

HOLMES

I am hoping to arrive at a solution to the Alexander murder.

WATSON

It is important to me. I have always wished I could see you perform even a small portion of one of the great roles of Shakespeare.

HOLMES

Well, I never require much persuading to perform ...

WATSON

Excellent. What about the soliloquy of Hamlet's where he has just seen a company of actors put on a moving scene, and it strikes him that while they are full of passion, he seems unaffected by his own father's murder --

HOLMES

The very thing. I know it well.

> He takes a moment to
> prepare, then presents
> himself as the melancholy
> and self-tormenting prince.

HOLMES

"O, what a rogue and peasant slave am I! Is it not monstrous that this player here, but in a fiction, in a dream of passion, could force his soul so to his own conceit that from her working all his visage wann'd, tears in his eyes, distraction in's aspect, a broken voice, and his whole function suiting with forms to his conceit? And all for nothing! For Hecuba! What's Hecuba to him, or he to Hecuba, That he should weep for her?

> Hamlet's confusion gives way
> to a torrent of righteous
> anger --

HOLMES

"What would he do, had he the motive and the cue for passion That I have? He would drown the stage with tears and cleave the general ear with horrid speech, make mad the guilty and appall the free, confound the ignorant, and amaze indeed the very faculties of eyes and ears.

>   -- then back to his inner
>   maelstrom of self-loathing --

HOLMES

"Yet I, a dull and muddy-mettled rascal, peak, Like John-a-dreams, unpregnant of my cause, and can say nothing; no, not for a king, upon whose property and most dear life a damn'd defeat was made. Am I a coward? Who calls me villain? Breaks my pate across? Plucks off my beard, and blows it in my face? Tweaks me by the nose? Gives me the lie i' the throat, as deep as to the lungs? Who does me this?

>   -- which boils over into a
>   vision of violent revenge on
>   his murderous uncle:

HOLMES

"Ha! 'Swounds, I should take it: for it cannot be but I am pigeon-liver'd and lack gall to make oppression bitter, or ere this I should have fatted all the region kites with this slave's offal: bloody, bawdy villain! Remorseless, treacherous, lecherous, kindless villain! O, vengeance!"

>   Watson applauds. Holmes is
>   surprised by the sound -- he
>   stands motionless, confused,
>   the imaginary dagger still in
>   his hand and wet with the
>   blood of the treacherous
>   uncle on whom he has
>   wrought his vengeance.

WATSON

As I always suspected.

> Holmes hears Watson's voice
> but it appears to come from
> far away --

HOLMES

I don't ... I ...

WATSON

A stirring performance. Surely it must have drawn
deeply on some vast reserve of ... what would you call
it?

HOLMES

I wonder if I might, ah --

WATSON

It's odd, since everyone knows strong feelings of any
kind are repugnant to you.

HOLMES

Watson.

WATSON

Yet surely a man of stone could not summon up
passions as deep as these.

HOLMES

Watson, I recognize that I am human. I have never
pretended to be otherwise. I simply find it more --

WATSON

You always used to say that emotion clouds reason,
and therefore was to be avoided at all times. I have
seen you put that into practice, you clearly believe it to
be true.

HOLMES

I do.

WATSON

It allows Sherlock Holmes to be, for example, entirely immune to the charms of women.

HOLMES

Not ... entirely.

WATSON

Or to the possible harm that might come to him from taking any person into his confidence. To be forever safe from the threat of having a close friend.

HOLMES

What do you want me to say?

WATSON

I want you to be honest with me!

HOLMES

I have been perfectly honest! For me to be "dead" for three years, it was absolutely imperative that you be among those deceived.

An awful silence.

HOLMES

I did return to England with some expectation that you would be pleased to resume our old partnership. But if you think it best that you continue on your own ... if you prefer to devote your full energies to your medical practice ...

WATSON

In other words, to continue my life as it is? As it has been for three years?

                              Holmes has no answer for
                              this. Finally:

                    HOLMES
I should try to sleep. Must be nearly midnight.

                              From far away, cathedral
                              chimes ring out the hour.

                    WATSON
Another theory confirmed.

                    HOLMES
The old cathedral ... I had almost forgotten ...

                    WATSON
What about it?

                    HOLMES
I have always been ... sensitive to sounds. Music.
Voices. Cathedral chimes. How many nights I have
sat in this beloved old chair, musing over some
complex problem of logic, when those chimes would
proclaim the midnight hour. Sometimes I would look
out and see, even in the darkness, the faint outline of
the church's spires. Ghostly, inscrutable shapes, they
always seemed to me and yet -- reassuring. They had
always been there and, I felt, always would be.

                    WATSON
Well. Much has changed in the old city since you left.
But I know it is still possible to see --

                              Watson pulls back a drape --

                              -- and one pane of the
                              window explodes in a spray
                              of glass shards. At the same

                                        instant, Holmes flings
                                        himself at Watson, knocking
                                        him to the floor.

                                        Holmes gropes for the
                                        draw-cord and pulls the
                                        drapes closed.

                          HOLMES
You truly are the most dim-witted man on earth.

                          WATSON
I'll not deny it. That was remarkably stupid. But at
least I had the satisfaction of seeing you proved wrong.

                          HOLMES

Wrong?

                          WATSON
You said Colonel Moran never misses.

                          HOLMES
I'm sorry to disappoint you. He never does.

                                        Holmes opens his robe to
                                        reveals the stream of blood
                                        trailing down from his heart.

                                        He faints into Watson's
                                        arms.

End of Act One

Jack Cannon as Holmes in the original production at the
University of Alabama at Birmingham

Jack Cannon as Holmes and Alan Gardner as Watson in the
University of Alabama at Birmingham production

Alan Gardner as Watson and Lee Shackleford as Holmes in the off-Broadway production

D.C. Cathro as Holmes and David Norman as Watson in the premiere of the newly-revised script at the New Play House in Frederick, Maryland

The *Hamlet* scene: Alan Gardner and Lee Shackleford
in the 2001 Library Theatre production

Stage left detail, Kel Laeger's 221B set for the Library
Theatre production

Stage right detail, Kel Laeger's 221B set for the Library
Theatre production

Full set of the 2001 Library Theatre production. Scenic, lighting, and property design by Kel Laeger.

Act Two

ACT TWO

Scene One

No time has passed.

WATSON

Holmes! Holmes ... your eyes glazed over for a second, and I thought ...

HOLMES

My -- my whole life was passing before my eyes, just as in the novels.

WATSON

Let me get you to the chair.

> Watson helps Holmes to a
> seat, where they strip off
> Holmes' robe and waistcoat
> then tear open his shirt-front
> to better reveal the wound.
> Watson examines the injury.

WATSON

The bullet has definitely lodged in your body.

HOLMES

So I gathered.

WATSON

Removing it could be extremely painful.

HOLMES

At the moment I find it difficult to imagine the
extraction of this bullet being any more painful than
its insertion.

WATSON

Painful and dangerous. If the bullet has struck an
artery, then its removal may result in internal bleeding
-- bleeding I would be unable to suppress.

HOLMES

Is it not more likely that this foreign object is causing
more damage the longer it remains and therefore
should be removed at once, regardless of any other
risk?

WATSON

I ... I agree. Yes. Fortunately, you are already
somewhat anaesthetized. Unfortunately ... so am I.
Now, you'll have to apply steady pressure here -- just
keep pressing right there. I have to get my -- uh --

> Watson hurries to his room
> and collects his water-basin.
> Holmes stares dreamily into
> space.

WATSON

Do you suppose that the police were alerted to Moran's
position by that rifle shot? Holmes?

HOLMES

"'tis not so deep as a well, nor so wide as a church-door; but 'tis enough, 'twill serve ... "

WATSON

Holmes?

HOLMES

Romeo and Juliet. Act Three, Scene One.

WATSON

I know.

HOLMES

Very good.

WATSON

I said, do you think Moran has given himself away?

HOLMES

Almost certainly. So you might say that our work here is finished. Pity that I may be finished as well ...

WATSON

Nonsense. We'll have this out and then we'll know if you require further surgery. But I will have to go down to the kitchen for water.

HOLMES

Don't show your face at any of the windows on the way down.

WATSON

I won't. While I am gone, you have some more brandy.

HOLMES

Well, if that's the prescription of my doctor.

Watson goes. Holmes rises
painfully and crosses to the
brandy bottle. His brave
pretense of being immune to
the pain drops. The wound
is clearly agonizing.

He eyes the box from
Alexander. He ponders. He
decides. He takes out one of
the bottles, crosses to the
deal-top chemistry table. He
measures out a small
amount of the fluid and
dissolves it in a beaker of
water. From his desk he
removes a leather case which
contains a hypodermic
syringe. He dips the needle
into the beaker and draws
the solution into the syringe.
Slowly and steadily, he
injects the fluid under the
skin of his wrist. Then he
removes the needle, drops it
back into its case, and sinks
back into his chair with a
long sigh.

At this moment Watson
returns, with his basin and
cloths.

WATSON
For once you had the good sense to remain still.

Watson checks the wound.

                    WATSON
Appears the bleeding's stopped.

                              He looks closer.

                    WATSON
Completely stopped. Almost as if your entire
circulatory system had suddenly constricted.

                              He examines Holmes' pupils.

                    WATSON
Very much like the effects of cocaine, that. Very much
indeed. I'd say a subcutaneous injection, a solution of
five-to-ten per cent --

                    HOLMES
This was a medical emergency.

                    WATSON
Holmes, cocaine makes a very poor anaesthetic. I
should imagine it would have the effect of heightening
sensation rather than lessening it.

                    HOLMES
I was endeavoring to control this bleeding and you
must admit I have been successful.

                    WATSON
You have made your suffering worse, and you will
suffer even more greatly later when the inevitable
depression follows.

                              Holmes' hands twitch
                              nervously now, and when he
                              speaks his words come
                              spilling out in a mad rush.

                              Meanwhile Watson cleans
                              the wound and probes for
                              the bullet.

                    HOLMES
Nonsense -- I have taken cocaine frequently with no ill
effects whatever -- or when there have been ill effects
-- and indeed there have been times when there were
so I should not have said there were none -- on those
occasions -- what was I saying? Why do you stand
there staring -- are you going to remove this bullet, or
shall I do it?

                    WATSON
It is very tempting to sit here and watch you try it.
Fortunately for you, I have always faithfully kept my
Hippocratic Oath.

                    HOLMES
                    (chattering away)
I have never attempted self-surgery, it could be very
interesting -- in practical application of course it would
be extremely instructive. I used to do this -- not
remove bullets from myself -- but explore human
tissue -- my self-directed education in criminal
investigation -- at St. Bartholomew's they used to allow
me to examine the occasional cadaver -- very
instructive, priceless experience -- I remember one --

                    WATSON
Holmes.

                    HOLMES
Yes?

                    WATSON
Shut up.

                              76

                    Holmes falls into a sulky
                    silence. Watson completes
                    his exploration and prepares
                    a formidable pair of forceps.

                 WATSON
I have located the bullet. I believe it can be removed
without further damage to blood vessels. I should say
you were very lucky.

                 HOLMES
Well, not very lucky -- after all, I did get shot.

                    Holmes laughs at his own
                    remark as if it were the
                    funniest joke ever made --
                    but his laughter jerks to a
                    stop when Watson reaches
                    into the wound with the
                    forceps.

                 WATSON
Let me know the moment you experience any
discomfort.

                 HOLMES
Thank you, I will.

                    Watson rotates the forceps,
                    struggling to gain a better
                    grip on the bullet. Holmes
                    struggles with the temptation
                    to cry out, writhe, or faint.

                 HOLMES
I do wish you'd be careful -- I believe you are very close
to my carotid artery.

WATSON

That is not the carotid.

HOLMES

Are you certain? I have made a rather thorough study -- ah! Old fellow, I do believe you're enjoying this.

WATSON

Let us say that I think your suffering is well-deserved.

HOLMES

I don't suppose it would be sporting to mention that I sustained this injury while saving your life.

WATSON

Is that what you call it?

HOLMES

Watson, I was pushing you away from the bloody window.

WATSON

It all happened so quickly, I -- well. I am grateful to you for that.

HOLMES

You must admit I am capable of self-sacrifice.

WATSON

The very reason why you are a hero to millions.

HOLMES

Am I indeed?

WATSON

Well, of course you are, Holmes -- otherwise nobody would tolerate you.

At last the bullet comes free.
Watson applies pressure to
the wound as he holds the
metal slug up for Holmes to
see.

HOLMES

Fascinating.

WATSON

Would you like to keep this?

HOLMES

Perhaps you'd like to add it onto your watch-chain.

WATSON

I think not.

HOLMES

No, you're right; it is material evidence. We must add
it to the collection at Scotland Yard.

WATSON

There is no further bleeding. That is a blessed relief.

HOLMES

Oh, so there was no arterial damage after all? Even
after all of your -- excavation?

Holmes staggers to his feet.

WATSON

For God's sake, Holmes, sit down.

HOLMES

But I feel perfectly fit.

WATSON

That's euphoria! I'm surprised you're even conscious.

HOLMES

Aren't you supposed to sew this up or some such
thing?

WATSON

No -- since no major vessels seem to have been
damaged, dressing and a bandage will suffice. But I
have no intention of chasing you around the room to
do it!

> Holmes sits, chastised.
> During the following, Watson
> cleans the area and ties a
> compress to Holmes' upper
> chest.

WATSON

Almost no bleeding at all, yet your blood pressure is
up. Hard to imagine what this is doing to your
cardio-vascular system.

HOLMES

You really should try it, Watson -- even the weakest
solution of cocaine sends lightning-flashes of energy
surging through your brain!

WATSON

It sends blood rushing to your head! That is all.

HOLMES

Whatever the reason, its effect is so -- so clarifying, so
electrifying --

WATSON

Someday there will be laws against it and all who abuse this chemical will be punished as criminals.

HOLMES

I suppose that is intended to frighten me. And I told you I am not an habitual user. True, in the old days, I resorted to cocaine when there were no problems on hand to stimulate my brain cells -- I had to seek artificial means --

WATSON

A very poor excuse. Well. This should hold the compress in place for the rest of the night. If you will remain still. Tomorrow we'll go to my office and bandage it all up more properly.

HOLMES

Why wait until tomorrow? Oh, you mean once Moran is behind bars? I expect he has already been apprehended. I think I shall go out and make certain of this. Hand me my hat and coat, old fellow.

WATSON

I will do nothing of the kind.

HOLMES

I beg your pardon?

WATSON

I will not be an accessory to your further self-destruction.

HOLMES

Oh dear.

WATSON

If you want my opinion, the only thing you should do
now is to sit quietly and wait for that drug to run its
course.

HOLMES

That is your expert medical opinion, is it?

WATSON

It is. Not that I expect you to heed it. You have not
been prone to accepting my advice in the past.

HOLMES

Not when it contradicts my knowledge and experience.

WATSON

And your knowledge and experience now suggests that
you should go out in the middle of the night, with a
hastily bandaged bullet-wound in your chest and a
bloodstream brimming with cocaine.

HOLMES

Do you know, I have survived the absence of doctors
very well in the last three years. I am perfectly capable
of taking care of myself.

WATSON

So I can see.

HOLMES

You really expect me to simply sit here and do nothing.

WATSON

Why not spend the time telling me about your
adventures of the last three years? And, if you like,
conclude with an explanation of your reasons for
returning.

Holmes tries to ignore this,
but the agitation of the
cocaine is slipping away. He
is beginning the inevitable
slide into depression.

HOLMES

Do you remember once trying to get me to read one of
those adventure stories you seem to enjoy so much -- a
bit of frivolity from that Frenchman, ah, Jules Verne --

WATSON

Oh, yes. *Around the World in Eighty Days.*

HOLMES

That's the one. Well, you know I don't read such
things --

WATSON

You might enjoy that novel. It is the story of a brilliant
Englishman who continually underestimates the
worthy companion on whom he is dependent.

HOLMES

Be that as it may. I was tempted by that notion of
circumnavigating the globe. My journey required a
good deal more than eighty days, but then I was in no
hurry to return.

WATSON

So you have been around the world! Holmes, surely
you had experiences worth relating -- saw marvels
most men never --

HOLMES

If it gives you any idea of what my travels were like, I
spent the better part of one year in a chemical
laboratory in Montpelier researching derivatives of
coal-tar.

WATSON

You spent a year experimenting with tar.

HOLMES

Yes. So much for your thrilling adventures. But I
have returned home and I should think that would be
sufficient for you.

WATSON

I do believe that is the first time I have ever heard you
refer to Baker Street as your "home."

HOLMES

Nonsense ... not a half hour ago you heard me
rhapsodizing over the cathedral chimes that are so
much a part of the *genius loci* -- the spirit of this place.

WATSON

That is not the same thing.

HOLMES

I don't see why not.

WATSON

It is significant that you volunteered the word itself.

HOLMES

You are splitting hairs, old fellow. A remark such as
that gives you away as an author. And here you are
pretending to be a doctor.

WATSON

I have enjoyed some success as both, thank you very
much.

HOLMES

Since you brought it up, I have been intending to ask
you what new accomplishments have jeweled your
crown since I saw you last.

WATSON

What do you mean?

HOLMES

Are you still reaping the benefits of being my
chronicler, of making palatable and popular our grisly
excursions into the criminal?

WATSON

You might say that I am. I do write other things as
well.

HOLMES

This is the first I have heard of it.

WATSON

Some of my work has actually attracted some artistic
acceptance.

HOLMES

Ah. Poetry, no doubt.

WATSON

Some of my published work has been poetic, yes.

HOLMES

I might have known. But you have devoted most of
your energies to the reports of our criminal
investigations.

WATSON

Oh, yes. The public clamors for more, always for more. "Tell us another story about Sherlock Holmes!"

HOLMES

I've noticed you've never bothered to tell them story of my final battle with Professor Moriarty. And I've noticed our stalwart London newspapers never ran my obituary.

WATSON

Through no fault of mine. You should know I spent many a day campaigning for your demise to be given the proper attention. But always the answer came back, "When you present us with a body, Dr. Watson, we will pronounce the poor fellow dead." Until that time you were considered merely missing.

HOLMES

Rubbish. You said there was general mourning throughout the city.

WATSON

Oh, there were many who grieved, certainly. In the spring of 1891 I could not walk a mile in the heart of the city without meeting someone wearing a black armband, eager to give me his condolences.

HOLMES

Well, that is gratifying at least.

WATSON

But not official. And I must say, there were many more who had not heard of your passing, and when they did ...

HOLMES

Yes?

WATSON

Surely you must know that throughout your career
you have left a trail of admirers behind you wherever
you went. Admirers -- but not friends.

HOLMES

And what of it? There are precious few human beings
whose company I do not find positively loathsome. I
have never made any attempt to conceal that fact.

WATSON

My point exactly.

HOLMES

I am compelled to agree with the great satirist
Jonathan Swift, who observed that mankind is "the
most pernicious race of little odious vermin that
Nature ever suffered to crawl upon the surface of the
earth." It was not my business to make friends with
people I dislike. It was my business to solve their
idiotic problems for them. It was my business to
stanch the rising tide of criminal activity in a city to
which the refuse of society seem drawn as carrion
crows to a rotting carcass.

WATSON

I'm sure you are aware, then, that criminal activity in
London is a good deal worse than three years ago.

HOLMES

And I am somehow to blame for this?

WATSON

You did say your reason for pretending to be dead was
so the criminal underworld would grow careless,
allowing their easy capture by the police.

HOLMES

You should not be surprised that our police have
bungled yet another opportunity --

WATSON

But if you had no confidence in the police, how could
you believe there was a purpose to be served in --

HOLMES

Watson, must we continue on this tiresome subject? I
grow immensely weary of this -- and indeed of
everything else.

WATSON

Ah, the aftereffect of the cocaine. Right on schedule.

HOLMES

I am well aware of the aftereffects of cocaine.

WATSON

I was merely reminding you that I warned you earlier.

HOLMES

Yes, your thoughtfulness is appreciated. Now for
God's sake, let's change the subject. Why don't you
read me one of the poems you bragged about earlier.

WATSON

I wasn't boasting, I was responding to --

HOLMES

Oh, never apologize for your own work, Watson, not if
you are to shine as an artist. There is little enough
solace in creativity without having to be sorry for what
one does. I have been able to reconcile much of my
work with my conscience only because I have ignored
the consequences of some of my actions. It has always
been this way with intelligent, creative people, and will

always be the same. This is why I resolved, long ago, never to apologize for anything. Nothing is worse than having to be sorry about one's work. Nothing!

WATSON
That's a very cynical attitude, Holmes.

HOLMES
It is a fact. I can see that the Creator Himself must have surely been in a black mood when He looked down upon the wicked people of Noah's time and was forced to repent that He had created them at all.

WATSON
I have noticed an alarming habit you have of comparing yourself with the Almighty. I have often wondered about that. I think it betrays some aspect of your character.

HOLMES
Don't be vulgar, Watson. The comparison is by no means absolute.

WATSON
And I was waiting for you to refer to the last three years or so as your death, burial, and resurrection.

HOLMES
That is not the sort of comment I would have thought worthy of you. Really! Now please read your poem, or whatever it was. Anything at all, Watson, we simply cannot allow the mood of this festive evening to slip.

WATSON
I have the perfect piece to read. I wrote it about three years ago.

HOLMES

Ah. Before ... or after ... ?

WATSON

After. Immediately after.

> Watson retrieves a sheet of
> paper from his desk. Holmes
> reclines in his favorite chair,
> steeples his fingers and
> half-closes his eyes.

HOLMES

I am all attention.

WATSON

"Some men find their friend of friends
In times of dark and danger near
They fight their foes together
And conquer their own fear.
Such a man grows older
And summons up his past
He wonders what was best in life
Numbers them, first to last.
My life unfolds before me
Thanks to the records I keep
My friend is here beside me
Tho' his body lies in the deep.
I cannot say why this friend has gone
I only know he's left me here alone
He planned to die for the good of all
And so he fought and took that fall
That robbed the world of a marv'lous mind
And left his friend, the trace to find.
How much more that friend would please
To set down better words than these
To praise that hero who has gone:
The best and the wisest man I've known."

Pause.

WATSON
I'm afraid poetry is probably not my great strength.

Silence. Then:

HOLMES
Well. I'm sure you'll agree it has been a long but diverting evening. I suppose it would harm neither of us to get some sleep. I shall see you in the morning, if you have not already left when I arise.

WATSON
I would value your response ... to the poem.

HOLMES
It is very interesting. The rhyme scheme is, I believe, somewhat unorthodox, and that is challenging. Some of the metrical notions are slightly strained, the rhymes uninventive. I'd have to examine the text to say more. Thank you for sharing it with me, though. I am very tired; I am sure I shall drop straight off to sleep. Good night.

> He goes, a bit too quickly for grace. Watson stands, looking at the closed door.
>
> After a moment, Watson walks away, looking at the page on which the poem is written. He crumples the page and hurls it with all his might at Holmes' door.
>
> He waits as if there might be a response from Holmes.

91

Then he heads for his own
room -- then just as he is
about to close the door
behind himself he stops.

Watson strides purposefully
to Holmes' door. He raises
his fist to knock --

-- and falters. He stands by
the door, at once hating
himself and Holmes, then
forces himself away to his
room and closes the door
behind him.

After a moment, Holmes'
door opens and a timid,
thick-bespectacled Anglican
clergyman enters, carrying a
large black Bible with a silver
cross on the cover.

                    HOLMES
Watson?

He moves quietly to the
center of the room.

                    HOLMES
Watson?

Satisfied he is alone, Holmes
crosses to the front door and
opens it -- then stops. He
looks back, torn.

His gaze falls on the Edison
recorder. Holmes makes his
decision. He closes the door,
and approaches the
machine. He inserts a
cylinder and starts the
motor.

HOLMES
My dear Watson. It is twelve-thirty now and the
depression you had predicted is upon me in full force.
But even here in the depth of hopelessness I feel an
obligation to making certain that Colonel Moran no
longer poses a threat to my life. Or, more importantly,
to yours. So I am going to confront him now, and
quite frankly do not expect to return. Since this may
be our last communication, I feel I should explain the
... very simple matter which I have allowed to become
so complicated. I said before that in the last three
years I had been around the globe. What I did not say
is that in those travels I met countless thousands of
people -- men and women of every caste and creed,
and in general I found the inhabitants of our world to
be a seething mass of cowards, bullies, hypocrites, and
warmongers. After three years of this it finally
occurred to me that the problem with the world is not
that there are too many unsolved crimes. The problem
is that there are too few people like John Watson.
Courageous. Honest. Considerate. Trustworthy.
Once I realized this, it seemed logical that I should
return to the company of the only person I ... the only
person who is like you. And to hope and pray that you
would welcome me back as your friend.
(A beat, then)
Whatever happens to me now I hope you will
remember me as... your greatest admirer, Sherlock
Holmes.

Holmes removes the cylinder
and places it next to the one
Watson had discarded
earlier. He approaches
Watson's door, and utters a
quiet benediction.

HOLMES

"Good night, sweet Prince ... and flights of angels sing
thee to thy rest."

He turns to go, then --

HOLMES

That's from *Hamlet*. Act Five, Scene Two.

And with that, he quietly
opens the front door and
vanishes into the night.

Scene Two

Daylight floods through the
windows, muted by the
still-closed drapes. Silence,
except for the faraway
clip-clop of a carriage on the
street below.

Silence.

From Holmes' room, a
tremendous crash of broken
glass, followed by the sound
of a body falling to the floor.

Holmes' door opens. Holmes,
still dressed as the priest,
staggers in from his room.
He clutches his bullet-wound
in agony, one arm almost
entirely useless now. He
barely manages to hang onto
his Bible -- and to the
tattered copy of the *Times* he
clutches in one trembling
hand.

                    HOLMES
Watson ...

                              He looks around in vain for
                              his friend. Holmes sees the
                              door to Watson's room is
                              closed. Summoning all his
                              strength, he tries to shout
                              but falters.

                    HOLMES
Watson!

                              He steadies himself against a
                              table, catching his breath.
                              He sees Watson's medical
                              bag, left out from last night.
                              Holmes drags himself to the
                              bag, fumbles it open and
                              begins to dig through its
                              contents. He examines a
                              glass bottle.

                    HOLMES
... shall never understand why ... doctors must write in
their own ... secret cipher ...

                              Failing to find what he seeks,
                              Holmes abandons the bag
                              and returns to where he left
                              his Bible.

                    HOLMES
It is past time I called upon a power greater than my
own.

                              Holmes reaches for the book
                              with apparent reverence --

> --then opens it to reveal a
> hole cut into the center of
> the pages -- and in the hole,
> a pistol. Holmes removes the
> gun, pulls back its trigger,
> and points the barrel at the
> ceiling. He fires.
>
> Watson's door flies open.
> Watson stands in the
> doorway, eyes wide and
> shirttails untucked.

HOLMES

Good morning.

> Watson looks around the
> room, dazed.

WATSON

Did someone just fire ... ?

HOLMES

Yes. I did. Sorry.

WATSON

I see. And why ...?

HOLMES

Desperate to get ... your attention ...

WATSON

Why, what's -- have you -- ?

> He hurries to Holmes and
> finally sees the details of the
> disguise.

                    WATSON
Why on earth are you dressed as an Anglican
minister?

                    HOLMES
You prefer another denomination?

                              Watson exposes Holmes'
                              bullet wound -- and blanches
                              in horror at it.

                    WATSON
Good God. How long ago did this start bleeding again?

                    HOLMES
No idea ...

                    WATSON
This wound should have contracted -- if anything it
appears to have expanded --

                    HOLMES
I shouldn't be surprised.

                    WATSON
There really is little else I can do for you here. We
shall have to go to my office -- or to a hospital.

                    HOLMES
First ... hoping to find something for ... pain ...

                    WATSON
Oh dear. All I carry is morphine --

                    HOLMES
Excellent --

WATSON

-- but I fear I am all out at the moment.

HOLMES

Ah. No wonder I ... couldn't find it.

WATSON

I am sorry. Perhaps more brandy ...

HOLMES

Brandy is absolutely the last thing I want.

WATSON

I see what you mean. Was it my imagination, or did
we drink a great deal last night?

HOLMES

If not, you have an excellent imagination.

WATSON

Then I fear I can do nothing else to ease your pain.
And you'll forgive me if I seem unsympathetic, but you
have clearly brought this added suffering on yourself.

HOLMES

I am aware of that.

WATSON

I assume that after I went to sleep you decided to face
Colonel Moran despite extreme exhaustion and fatigue,
a large amount of alcohol and cocaine in your
bloodstream, and a bullet-hole in your chest.

HOLMES

It seemed the logical course of action, yes.

WATSON

You really should be locked up for your own
protection.

HOLMES

You should have seen me a few moments ago. The
image of a man of the cloth climbing a rain-spout
one-handed, and then breaking in through my window
must have been an entertaining one.

WATSON

Breaking into --

HOLMES

Well, when I left here last night I locked the front door
behind me. Didn't want anyone to come in and ...
disturb you.

WATSON

I thank you for that, at least. And so?

HOLMES

So?

WATSON

Colonel Moran?

HOLMES

Oh. Moran. Yes. Well, I am ... not certain of his
precise whereabouts.

WATSON

I don't understand.

HOLMES

I will explain later. First let me read you something
from the morning paper.

WATSON

Why on earth would I want you to do that?

HOLMES

As I suspected, there have been important new developments in the Alexander problem.

WATSON

Holmes, for God's sake, we've been through this, and it seems clear to me that you --

HOLMES

"Proceedings are already being arranged against Samson Menninger, butler to Mr. Benjamin Alexander, in the murder of his employer. At present Mr. Menninger has no attorney for his defense." This, of course, is hardly surprising. But a new revelation shows me that justice is moving swiftly in the wrong direction.

WATSON

All right, Holmes, what new revelation -- ?

HOLMES

Do you remember Jacob Freeman? The imports manager in South America? Among the notices from the business world we find this: "Mr. Jacob Freeman, currently supervising the Alexander line in Peru, will assume the control of the entire Alexander organization. He will meet with the board of directors tomorrow, etc., etc." Do you see? A sudden windfall of wealth and power for Jacob Freeman!

WATSON

You think Freeman murdered Alexander? How?

HOLMES

It does at least present a motive. And where there is a motive ... very often a method presents itself.

WATSON

We already know Freeman was trying to poison Alexander. He send him two crates of cocaine.

HOLMES

I catch the subtle drift of your satire, Watson. But there was no indication in the report that Alexander had recently sampled his cocaine when the murder took place.

WATSON

No specific mention of it, I know, and yet ...

HOLMES

You have reason to believe otherwise?

WATSON

Only a vague suspicion.

HOLMES

Not very scientific.

WATSON

I didn't say it was.

HOLMES

If a syringe had been found in the room it would surely have been mentioned in the report. Now, he might have taken the cocaine without the injection...

WATSON

You mean, eh, nasally?

HOLMES

Yes.

WATSON

Not the usual method. I've heard of people doing it,
though.

HOLMES

Yes, it's rather déclassé, but it is done on the
Continent, in America, in Australia. Some sort of tube
is usually employed. But there is also no mention of a
tube of any description on the murder scene.

WATSON

Well, there you are, then. Now if you're quite through
carrying on about this murder, will you please tell me
what has become of Moran and when we might be able
to leave this building?

Pause.

HOLMES

Moran is ... in custody. Owing to my clever disguise I
was able to quietly join the curious onlookers lining
the street as the local constabulary carted the
gentleman away.

WATSON

Then why in God's name did you tell me you didn't
know where he was?

HOLMES

I said I did not know precisely. Which is perfectly true.
They took him away, and I presume it was to prison,
but his exact location at this moment --

WATSON

Holmes, really.

HOLMES

So you see you are perfectly safe to come and go as you please. I cannot keep you here against your will.

WATSON

Though you do seem to be attempting to do so.

HOLMES

Nonsense. Why on Earth would I do that?

WATSON

I have no idea. So I ... I suppose I should be going.

HOLMES

I understand.

WATSON

Your ... injury will heal itself if you will only take my advice and rest here. You really should stay just as you are for as long as possible.

HOLMES

I have no intention of ever stirring from this spot.

WATSON

Well, then.

HOLMES

Yes.

WATSON

You do know ... I mean ...I can scarcely express my delight at finding you alive and well ... but it seems we are at a definite ... personal ... impasse.

HOLMES

If that is your opinion.

                    WATSON
I wish it were not so.

                    HOLMES
As do I.

                              A very uncomfortable pause.
                              Holmes nervously puts his
                              free hand in his pocket. He
                              finds the five-pound note
                              from the previous night.

                    HOLMES
Oh ... I believe this is yours.

                    WATSON
Ah, yes, thank you.

                         Pause.

                    WATSON
Well. I will see you soon, I assume.

                    HOLMES
Of course. No reason to pretend we don't know one
another.

                    WATSON
No, of course not.

                              He wraps the note around
                              his index finger, fidgeting.

                    WATSON
Well.

>He starts toward the door,
reaching for his hat. But at
the same moment, he looks
at the note around his finger.
He stops.

WATSON

Holmes! The hundred-pound note! We were
assuming Alexander had been holding it flat!

>Watson holds up the note,
twists it into a tighter tube.
He holds this tube up to his
nostril --

HOLMES

Good Lord --

WATSON

It may not make any difference, but ...

HOLMES

It may make all the difference, Watson! All the
difference in the world!

>He tries to sit up but is
stopped by the inevitable jolt
of pain.

HOLMES

The -- the bottles -- Alexander's gift --

WATSON

What about them?

HOLMES

Would you be so kind as to take them to my chemistry
table?

                    WATSON
Certainly ...

                         Watson hurries to comply --

          HOLMES
You'll find a bottle labeled "alkaline reactant --"

                    WATSON
Yes --

          HOLMES
Three graduated cylinders -- fill them halfway --

                    WATSON
                    (as he does this)
Yes ... and then, the cocaine? Will it be added -- ?

          HOLMES
Pour the powder into one of the cylinders.

                    WATSON
What will happen?

          HOLMES
A reaction will result.

                    Watson hesitates.

                    WATSON
Holmes ... the many scars on this table are ... grim
reminders ... of experiments you have conducted
which proved ... volatile ...

          HOLMES
For Heaven's sake, Watson, if you're afraid -- !

                         107

> Watson drops the powder
> into the cylinder. The liquid
> changes colors.

                    HOLMES

Aha!

                    WATSON

What does it mean?

                    HOLMES

It means it is cocaine.

                    WATSON

We knew that.

                    HOLMES

Yes, but now try another bottle.

> Watson repeats the
> experiment, and again the
> fluid changes color in the
> same way.

                    WATSON

What are we attempting to prove?

                    HOLMES

Remember that Alexander split his shipment with me
exactly. The fact that ours is clearly in its original
wrapping paper suggests that he had asked Freeman
to prepare them in this way. Freeman had no
knowledge that one was to be a gift to me. So if he had
been up to some foul play, he would have prepared
them both with the same arrangement of contents.

                    WATSON

Yes.

HOLMES

So -- we have a unique opportunity! Fate has placed
in our hands a clue that no one else could have.

WATSON

And if Alexander had been using his for three years ...
let us duplicate his usage by drawing a sample --

HOLMES

-- from the bottom of the box.

                              Watson digs through the
                              carton to get at a bottle near
                              the bottom. Then he repeats
                              the experiment -- and again
                              the fluid changes color -- but
                              this time the change is to a
                              sickening color, an essence
                              of evil. This new horror
                              froths and foams. Watson
                              puts it down and backs away
                              as if it might bite him.

WATSON

What was it?

HOLMES

Not cocaine.

WATSON

So I gathered.

HOLMES

Not even in the same family of vegetable alkaloids.

WATSON

Good Lord. Then Alexander ingested -- just like --

HOLMES

"Just like?"

WATSON

I once saw a man, similarly addicted, given the wrong drug during treatment ... he went into violent seizures -- and that man ... strangled, Holmes. I recall vividly that poor creature clutching at his own throat with horrible strength. He clawed at himself, trying to clear his own passage for a breath of air. And we were helpless. We tried to give him some relief, but his throat was closing up from inside.

HOLMES

Are you saying you believe this is what happened to Alexander?

WATSON

It would explain the marks on the throat, which have been previously attributed to the butler choking him. Yes. My medical opinion is that the injuries were made with his own hands.

HOLMES

And the poor butler, Menninger ... arrived just in time to see his master choke to death before his very eyes ... and to appear responsible.

WATSON

Jacob Freeman planned his employer's murder three years ago and has been biding his time ever since -- perhaps believing the time interval would allay suspicions about him.

HOLMES

Ah ... but the "1812 Overture" on the gramophone? There you have left out a factor. Where does it relate to the problem?

WATSON

You have said yourself that music seems far more
enjoyable under the spell of cocaine. Alexander was
enjoying his recreation ... and it killed him.

HOLMES

Yes. It does seem to cover all the facts ...

Pause.

HOLMES

And I would have eventually partaken from that bottle
myself.

Holmes shakes himself free
of this vision. He extends his
free arm to Watson.

HOLMES

Help me up, old fellow. We haven't a moment to
waste.

WATSON

Holmes, I told you --

HOLMES

I know, I know -- but now we have a crisis on hand.
This evidence may turn the tide for our friend the
hapless butler.

WATSON

Well ---

Watson reluctantly helps
Holmes to his feet.

HOLMES
Perhaps the guilty party may even be apprehended.
You and I must both go at once to Scotland Yard to
explain to the authorities how you've solved the
mystery!

WATSON
Oh, really, Holmes, I don't believe anyone could say --

HOLMES
Certainly! You observed the pound-note, the
strangling, the bit of your medical background that
proved --

WATSON
But you recognized the possibility that the cocaine was
in fact poisoned --

WATSON	HOLMES
-- without which this supposition would have been -- simply --	It was your hypothesis that -- it was the first workable theory --

They stop.

WATSON
Perhaps ... we could agree ... that we did this together?

HOLMES
Of course. As ... as we always did.

WATSON
Yes.

HOLMES
As we always will.

                        WATSON
Yes.

                        HOLMES
Yes. Now -- we must go! We'll need the
packing-crate and all the bottles.

                        WATSON
Of course.

                                    On his way across the room
                                    Watson notices the
                                    recording-cylinder Holmes
                                    left behind earlier. He picks
                                    it up as if he could identify it
                                    by sight.

                        WATSON
That's odd. I don't recall leaving ...

                                    Holmes hurries to snatch the
                                    cylinder from Watson.

                        HOLMES
Oh, that's a little something of mine. I'll ... buy you
another blank cylinder. But now --

                                    Holmes shoves the cylinder
                                    into his trouser pocket.

                        WATSON
When did you ... ? Could we hear it?

                        HOLMES
Oh, no, I don't think so. No.

                        WATSON
You're hiding something.

HOLMES

Watson, we are in haste. We can take up this
discussion when we return!

WATSON

Give me the cylinder, Holmes.

HOLMES

Watson!

WATSON

Then tell me what it says.

HOLMES

It was only a message telling you I had gone out in
search of Colonel Moran.

WATSON

Then why are you hiding it?

HOLMES

Watson -- for Heaven's sake. A man must have some
secrets.

WATSON

I see. So everything that's happened since you
returned --all for naught. You have learned nothing
and will not change. The secrets, the lies. And I
assume, the continue use of that drug ... the same bad
habit that killed Alexander, I need hardly mention.

> Holmes picks up the beaker
> in which he mixed his
> cocaine solution. It is still
> mostly full. He sets it on the
> fireplace mantle.

HOLMES

Ah, yes. About that. Look, since you happen to be
near your old service revolver, would you lend it to me
for a moment?

WATSON

Certainly, but why ... ?

> Watson hands him the
> pistol.

HOLMES

My resolution for the year to come.

> He shoots the bottle at
> point-blank range, sending a
> spray of liquid across the
> fireplace.
>
> Holmes calmly hands the
> pistol back to Watson.

HOLMES

And you will see that on this matter, my word is my
bond. Now, if you will be good enough to remove the
majority of the unpleasantness from any record you
may make of this particular case, we shall consider the
matter closed.

WATSON

I have no desire to write a story based on the last
twelve hours.

HOLMES

No. Our solution to the Alexander murder was arrived
at through most unorthodox methods.

                    WATSON
I quite agree.

                              Holmes takes down the
                              deerstalker and the
                              Inverness, drapes the coat
                              around his shoulders.

                    WATSON
Still, the world must know of your escape from the
waterfall, from Moriarty -- and of the capture of
Colonel Moran ...

                    HOLMES
Use your imagination, old friend. Be creative. Lie.

                              He puts on the deerstalker
                              cap and opens the front door
                              -- but notices Watson is not
                              behind him. He turns to find
                              Watson smiling at him.

                    HOLMES
Why ...?

                    WATSON
Well, Holmes, it's ... all is just as it should be. After all
this time, here we are again.

                              Holmes cannot deny the
                              truth of what Watson says.
                              And the two proud Victorian
                              gentlemen relax their facades
                              and permit a brief embrace.

                    HOLMES
Let us be off then.

WATSON

In a moment.

                    Watson holds up the
                    cylinder, which he has
                    picked from Holmes' pocket
                    during the embrace. Holmes
                    is stunned.

                    Watson loads it into the
                    machine, drops the needle,
                    and:

WATSON'S VOICE

This is John H. Watson. The date is ... April 4th,
1894. This will be, uh ... the first of ...

                    Holmes and Watson turn
                    simultaneously toward the
                    remaining cylinder and race
                    to it --

                    -- and Holmes wins. He
                    holds the cylinder up for
                    Watson to see, then quickly
                    pockets it again.

HOLMES

Come, Watson, come! Time is of the essence!

                    He stops at the door.

HOLMES

The game is afoot -- again!

And Holmes hurries out,
singing the "1812" loudly.

Watson stands watching his
departing friend for a
moment. Then with a smile,
he gathers his hat and the
packing-case, and hurries
joyfully out, joining Holmes
in the wordless rendition of
"1812," their voices blending
as they go ...

Appendix

Overcoming the
Technical Challenges of
Holmes & Watson

This show makes some extraordinary demands on its production team. First and foremost of these is, of course, is in finding two performers with the skill and stamina required for ninety-plus minutes of thrust-and-parry repartee. Any two-man show is challenging simply in terms of the number of lines to be learned, but this one requires the navigation of an emotional slalom-course as well.

But the purely technical requirements of the show may also be a bit daunting. In particular, there are the Edison cylinder recorder, the bending fireplace poker, the three-part experiment with the cocaine bottles, and the climactic exploding beaker.

So this appendix is provided in the hopes of easing the burden on scenic and property designers. To begin with, a suggested set layout, based on Kel Laeger's scenic design for the Library Theatre production, is reproduced on the following page.

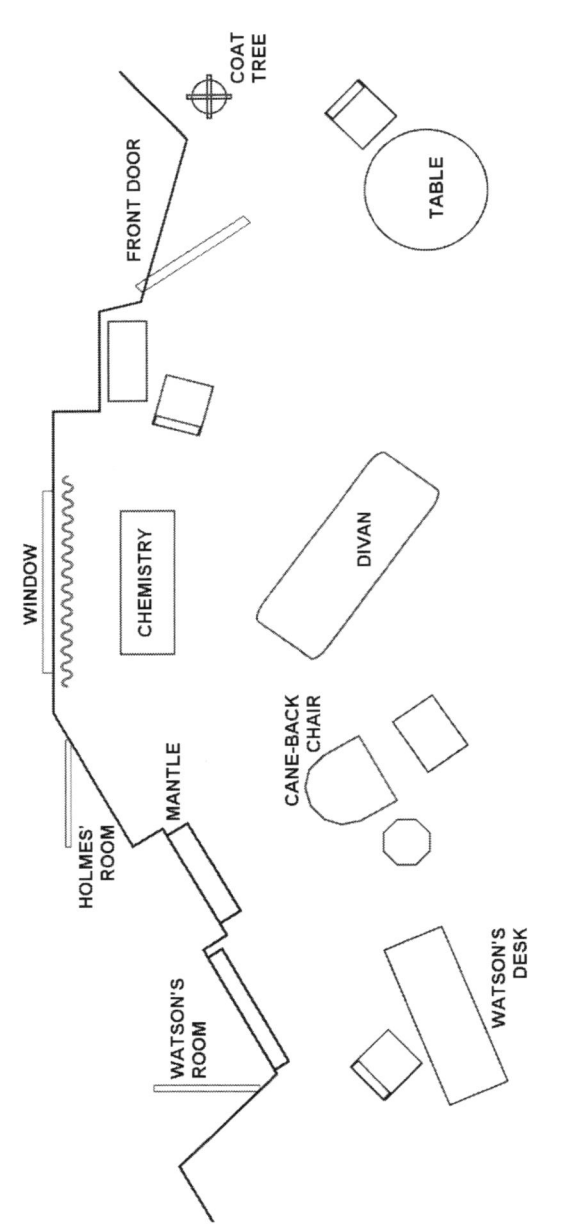

Some details of this set design are drawn from the depiction of 221B in the sixty original Sherlock Holmes stories by Sir Arthur Conan Doyle (most notably in "The Musgrave Ritual"). Many of these details are necessary because they are referred to in the script, but others may be desirable in any production designed to please Sherlockian purists in the audience.

A "canonically accurate" 221B setting must have, for example, an unframed photograph of Henry Ward Beecher and a framed photograph of Major-General Charles "Chinese" Gordon -- because they are specifically mentioned in the story "The Resident Patient." (In fact, a careful reading of the opening passages of that story will provide clues as to where the portraits should be located on the set.)
So photographs of Gordon and Beecher are included in this appendix, free to be scanned, enlarged, tinted sepia, and put to work as set pieces.

Productions of this play tend to attract people who are interested in various aspects of Victorian life, and so there will, for example, be handgun enthusiasts in the audience who can, in W. S. Gilbert's happy phrase, tell on sight a Mauser rifle from a javelin. Watson's gun was very likely a Webley such as the "British Bulldog," so a photograph of that gun is included here for reference.

Early in the script Holmes makes reference to Watson's stethoscope. The flexible stereo stethoscope familiar to all the world today was not in common use in Watson's day. His listening device would have been a simple cone or tube, three or four inches long. These were made of wood, rubber, or ivory and were sometimes carved or molded into "trumpet" shapes. A photograph of such a stethoscope is included here.

Major-General Charles George Gordon

Rev. Henry Ward Beecher

Watson's revolver, stethoscope, and recorder
(not to scale)

Special mention must be made of the all-important Edison Cylinder Recorder. The machine need not be a working model, fortunately, although many working specimens still exist. What is required, however, is that the audience can see the cylinders being exchanged on the spindle, and that there is some indication of when the needle is engaged and removed. The photograph included here should be of some help.

If the show has tended to attract experts on Victorian weapons, it has attracted still more people who know a lot about Victorian money. They will expect Watson's five-pound note, however fleetingly glimpsed, to look like the real thing. The necessary image has been included in this appendix; it needs only to be scanned and printed at 5" by 8.5" on one side of a high-rag-content white paper.

The fireplace poker has been approached many ways in different productions, but the method used by Kel Laeger in the off-Broadway production is almost certainly the best. He procured a cast-iron poker and cut a 6" section out of the middle of the shaft. These two ends were then inserted into a piece of copper tubing, the length of the original iron shaft. With modeling clay packed into the middle of the tube so the copper would not crimp when bent, the iron parts were inserted into the tube and soldered to the copper. When the entire assembly was painted matte black the result was a poker of convincing weight and heft -- one that made a satisfying "clang" when dropped -- but one which could be easily bent (and unbent) when needed.

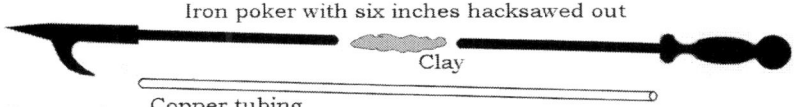

Iron poker with six inches hacksawed out

Clay

Copper tubing

Bank of England

A27 74339 to pay the Bearer on Demand

the Sum of Five Pounds

1881 Oct. 5   London 5 Oct. 1881

For the Gov.r and Comp.a of the
BANK of ENGLAND.

No Payment

Chief Cashier

A 2 7 4 3 9
125

Five

The cocaine experiment (pp. 107-109) has also been handled many ways over the years. In the earliest versions of the script, the powders were burned over an alcohol lamp, with the third mixture resulting in an ugly black cloud that hung over the set for the rest of the show. This was dramatically effective but sometimes annoying to the audience, and the entire procedure was in fact dangerous to the actors. In the New Play House production, director Jonah Knight suggested the experiment be done with fluids instead of fire, and after a quick rewrite this turned out to be a definite improvement on the earlier methods.

Chemistry teacher Karen Brinton then suggested further improvements to this approach. Her formula, reproduced below, uses ingredients available almost anywhere and yields wonderfully dramatic results.

Shopping List:
1 jug white vinegar
1 2 oz. bottle tincture of iodine
                    (2% iodine, not decolorized)
1 box table salt
1 bottle pure ascorbic acid, a.k.a. Vitamin C
                    (No chewables or added ingredients)
1 box corn starch
1 box baking soda (not baking powder)

Making the test solution:
This is the fluid that will be on Holmes' chemistry table throughout the show, ready for Watson to pour into three bottles for the experiment. Combine 1 cup of water with 1 cup of white vinegar, then stir in 1 tablespoon of iodine. The solution should be roughly the color of honey, and not so dark as to be opaque. Remember to always handle iodine with extreme caution -- it is poison and should be treated as such.

Making the "cocaine":

Using a mortar and pestle, grind the Vitamin C into a smooth, fine powder. Use 15 tablets if they are 1000 milligrams of Vitamin C; 30 if they are 500 milligrams. Add 1 cup of table salt and mix well. The mixture should be stored in tightly sealed bottles as described in the script.

Making the "poison":

Combine 1/4 cup of corn starch, 1/4 cup of baking soda, and 1/2 cup of table salt. Mix well and store in tightly sealed bottles.

The director and the actor playing Watson will need to experiment with the proportions to find the combinations which provide the desired results. But if a tablespoon of powder from the "cocaine" bottles is added to 1/8 cup of the iodine solution, the amber liquid will turn clear. Naturally the same thing will happen when this is repeated with the second "cocaine" bottle and the second vial of iodine solution. But when the powder from the third "cocaine" bottle -- the one pulled from the bottom of the Alexander package -- is added to the iodine solution, the amber liquid will not only fail to turn clear but will instead turn a rich purple-black, foaming and fizzing in a dramatically satisfying manner.

All of these ingredients are harmless -- except for the iodine, which can be fatal to humans even when diluted to 2% strength. So all precautions stated on the label of the iodine bottle should be followed to the letter. And when you dispose of the leftover mixture, remember that iodine may corrode pipes or harm the environment. The safest way to dispose of iodine is to "decolorize" it with vitamin C, exactly as described above, and to dilute it further with plenty of water.

Finally, the show's most complicated effect: the business where Holmes shoots the bottle on the mantlepiece. This effect has been handled in a wide variety of ways. One approach was an elaborate gimmick in which the actor playing Holmes placed the bottle on top of an explosive squib concealed in the top surface of the mantlepiece. The stage manager triggered the squib at the instant the actor playing Holmes fired the gun. This was extremely effective when both the squib and the gun fired on cue, but embarrassing when they did not. A less complex version involved a spring-loaded piston hidden in the mantlepiece, released when the gun was fired, sending the bottle flying. This was effective when breakaway glass was used, as the bottle would shatter on stage rather than flinging fragments -- or bouncing intact -- into the audience.

More often than not, however, actors playing Holmes have found they had to break the bottle with the butt of the revolver. This is a perfectly viable approach to the scene. All that is required is that Holmes make a typically outsized gesture which he feels demonstrates to Watson that he has renounced his dangerously bad habit. Of course it proves nothing of the kind; but it is a gesture intended to convince Watson (and the audience) -- so the more outlandish that gesture is, the more convincing this moment will be. It is vital that the audience believe Holmes is through with cocaine forever.

Endless Thanks

The success of this play over the years is owed to so many people, I can never properly thank them all. As Holmes says "We can but try." Thanks, then, to:

Kel Laeger
Jon Lellenberg, BSI
Gordon Speck, BSI
Wm. Cochran, BSI
Paul Singleton, BSI
Peter Blau, BSI
Andy Solberg, BSI
P.K. Jones
Bob Funk
Dr. Robert Yowell
Jack Cannon and Alan Gardner
Elizabeth Adkisson
Karen Brinton
Jonah and Lisa Knight
D.C. Cathro and David Norman

and to three who have gone beyond the Reichenbach:
Dr. Asimov, Jeremy Brett, and Bernard Block

and of course -- it almost goes without saying -- to
Sir Arthur Conan Doyle
for his intriguing characters
and for the situation presented in his story
"The Adventure of the Empty House"

but most of all ...
like Holmes himself, I owe everything to
the doctor with whom I share lodgings
and who continues to tolerate my eccentricities.

Lee Eric Shackleford
Spring 2007

Lee Eric Shackleford is the author of
over 100 produced scripts for
stage, screen, and radio. He is an
Active Member of the Dramatists Guild
and Playwright-in-Residence at the
University of Alabama at Birmingham.

His web site at
www.gulliver.cc
exists in a state of
perpetual evolution.

Printed in Great Britain
by Amazon.co.uk, Ltd.,
Marston Gate.